Russell's
Christmas
Magic

Rob Scotton

SCHOLASTIC INC.
New York Toronto London Auckland Sydney
Mexico City New Delhi Hong Kong Buenos Aires

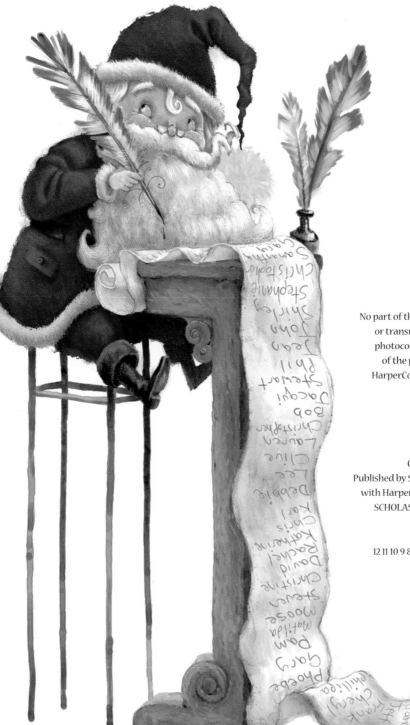

Special thanks to Maria

ISBN-13: 978-0-545-14083-6
ISBN-10: 0-545-14083-8

12 11 10 9 8 7 6 5 4 3 2 1   8 9 10 11 12 13/0

Printed in the U.S.A.   08

First Scholastic printing, November 2008

Typography by Martha Rago

For my family and yours

—R.S.

'TWAS the night before Christmas in Frogsbottom Field. Not a creature was stirring,

except for . . .

Russell. As he was hanging the very last lantern on the old tree, a shooting star caught his eye.

Closer and closer it came.

Brighter and brighter,

and then . . .

WHOOOSH!

The shooting star snuffed out the lanterns and came down somewhere in Firefly Wood.

"Now Christmas is ruined," Russell groaned . . .

and he trudged off to investigate.

He came upon a small, round man brushing snow from his belly.

"Santa!" Russell exclaimed.

"You see! You see!
You shouldn't see me," Santa said.
"The sleigh is broken, and so
is the Christmas Spell.

Christmas
must be
canceled!"

The sleigh was beyond repair.

"First Christmas is ruined, and now it's canceled," said Russell.

WHAT'S A SANTA TO DO?

An idea bounced around in Russell's hat and settled on his head.

He raced to his workshop,
grabbed his tool chest,
and headed for
a snowy mound.

Russell dug

and dug

until . . .

a rusty old car emerged.

"How can that help?" Santa asked, and sighed.

So Russell welded this part to that.

He hammered
and sawed

and
banged
and
clattered.

SANTA 1

Finally
he turned to Santa.

"Well?" Russell asked sheepishly.

"Russell, it . . . it's . . .
It's wondrous, magnificent—a thing
of beauty, a work of genius!" Santa gushed.

"Will it work?"

As Santa harnessed the reindeer to the new sleigh,
they began
to disappear.

"I can't see you!" said Russell.

"You see! You see!
You can't see me.
The sleigh is fixed, and so
is the Christmas Spell," cried Santa.

"Christmas
is uncanceled!"

"Will you come with us?" asked Santa.

"Will we be gone for long?" asked Russell.

"For the blink of an eye!" he replied.

Russell felt for the sleigh and climbed aboard.

"I can see you again," he said to Santa.

"Of course! Now you're part of the
Christmas Spell," cried Santa.

"Now, Dasher! Now, Dancer! Now, Prancer and Vixen!
On, Comet! On, Cupid! On, Donder and Blitzen!"

Up, up, higher and higher they flew.

Across land, across oceans they sped.

Through the magical Northern Lights they passed.

They visited all the children of the world
and left presents for each and every one.

In the blink of an eye they were back in Frogsbottom Field.
Santa waved his hand, and presents appeared.

Santa gave Russell the very last present.

Inside was a tiny glass bauble.

Russell hung the ornament on the tree,
where it flickered and glowed.

Soon it shone with all the brilliance of the Northern Lights.

"It's a little bit of the Christmas Spell, just for you," said Santa.
"And now it's time, it's time to go."

"Good-bye, Russell, the sheep that saved Christmas," cried Santa.

"And Merry Christmas to you!"